SHATTERED PAGES

A JOURNEY THROUGH MIND AND MEMORY

KHYATHI GUTHI

Made with ♥ on the Notion Press Platform
www.notionpress.com

To all the dust in space, no one cared until it turned into
a nebula.

Foreword

This novel, a work of pure fiction, springs from the depths of the author's imagination, conjuring characters and scenarios that are entirely the creation of that imagination.

At the heart of this tale is a young girl whose quest to submit an essay leads her through a series of profound incidents. Her journey explores themes of anxiety, depression, and psychological disorders, set in a world where individuals struggle to express the turmoil within themselves—a delicate balance between reality and dreams.

Please be aware that this story may provoke deep reflections on existence and sensitive emotions. It serves as a reminder that these fictional accounts approach delicate topics with care. I hope you find solace and insight without becoming entangled in the journey of our protagonist, Ellen.

1

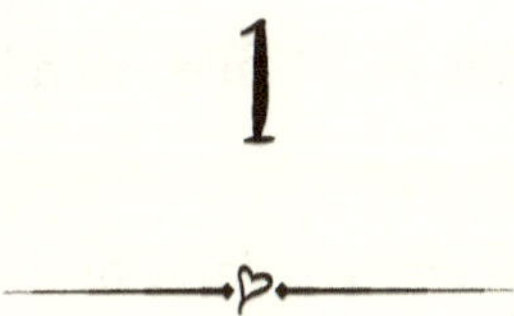

"Humans are the cruelest beings to ever exist. Snakes disguised as Doves, shedding crocodile tears, walk over streets leaving a mark of kindness when selfishness runs deep in their veins. It's like living in a game, a game called trust."

After reading, Marie slammed the book shut and glared at me, "This? Is this what you're planning to submit? Have you lost your mind? You're representing your school and state in this story writing competition. It's not some random school newspaper where you can write whatever you want!" She hurled the book to the ground. I stood still and didn't utter a word. My silence played a crucial role in this conversation with the principal, who happens to be my mother. I heard someone knock on the door, and my mother signaled me to leave. I picked up the book and walked to the door in silence.

"This conversation isn't over, Miss Ellen," she warned, her voice filled with anger as I exited. I simply walked away.

My name is Ellen Brown, a high schooler. To most people, I'm the quiet, introverted girl, the daughter of the school's principal, who expresses her thoughts through writing. I might be the invisible student to many, as I have no connections with many after school. It feels like an outcast living in this world, filled with lies and misplaced hope.

"Talking to yourself?" familiar voice asked from behind. I turned to see Casper.

"Nothing serious," I replied and I walked away. Casper was my classmate, more like the only person who talked to me. He's also my rival. As I was walking, my phone started to ring, frightening me in the tranquil hallway. I picked up the call.

"Hello, Uncle," I said.

"Dear, you haven't come, It's past your therapy time!" he said with concern.

"I'm on my way, Uncle," I replied and hung up the call.

I walked down the dimly lit hallways towards the therapy dorm, the sound of my footsteps echoing off the cold walls. My mother had insisted on me having therapy after reading some of my works. To my surprise, my therapist was none other than my uncle James. Both my mother and uncle were amazed by my writing and wanted me to enroll in many competitions. I have a lifelong passion for psychology.

Many things have frightened me recently. Someone stole my work and submitted it to the Story-Writing competition taking place nationwide. To my fear, I made it to the final level. I received an email with the topic for the final round: *"Humans, their beyond thoughts."*

I knocked on the door of the therapy dorm.

"Come in dear," Uncle James called to me from inside. I entered and took a seat on the couch nearest to me. "How is your writing going, dear?" He asked. I didn't respond immediately. Instead, I placed my diary on the coffee table. I could grasp his sad smile while he took the diary and started to read; for a moment, he seemed at a loss for words.

"Dear, your writing is impressive and filled with amazing metaphors, but don't you think it focuses too much on the negatives?" he questioned, while his voice filled with concern.

"It felt pointless to compete when I'm not allowed to write from my perspective," I replied softly.

He fell silent for a moment before asking, "Are you interested in participating in the competition?"

"It wasn't me who submitted the work to the competition," I answered.

"See, dear, It's a fantastic opportunity to be part of such a competition. Your ideas were strong enough to get you to the final round. I suggest you make use of the most of the resources. And remember, you'll need to start preparing for university admissions from the upcoming year," He said.

"I want to write, but my mind is in turmoil. I just need a break from everything for a while," I stated.

"Then why don't you go on a trip alone?" he suggested. I was taken aback by his suggestion. My mother would never allow it.

"Don't worry, I will talk to my sister about it," he reassured me. I felt a rare sense of relief and happiness.

"Uncle, I have some work to finish. Can we continue this session later?" I asked, hoping for an early leave.

"Alright, dear," he agreed. I left the room. It felt like a crime to feel so good amidst everything. I was on my way home.

I was walking down a seemingly endless street, feeling a strange mix of guilt and happiness. I wasn't sure how to name this conflicting emotion. I heard footsteps that seemed to match the rhythm of my own, and when I turned, to my surprise I found Casper behind me.

"Are you trying to follow me?" I asked, not bothering to hide my irritation.

"I was actually eavesdropping on your conversation about you going on a trip alone," he replied with the eyes of an innocent child.

His words took me by surprise. "Trying to stalk me? I bet there were better people to stalk," I replied.

"I wasn't stalking. I just want to be a good friend," he said in the sweetest tone I had ever heard.

"And how do you plan to be a good friend?" I questioned him, genuinely curious.

"Well, I know you love reading," he began.

"Yeah, I love reading. So, what does that have to do with this conversation?" I asked, puzzled.

"I'm not sure which book to give you, but you can choose any book from the library across the street," He offered, though he seemed unsure.

I was stunned by his offer. Was he really suggesting I pick a book from the restricted library his father owns? I was over the moon by his words about visiting the restricted library.

"Hmm, okay," I said, doing my best to act calm while my mind was filled with excitement.

2

We reached the library, and I could hardly hide my excitement. Casper opened the doors, and the sight that greeted me was nothing short of an incredible library. As we walked through the rows of tall shelves, I made my way to the psychology section, eager to find some intriguing reads.

Casper followed closely and asked, "Where are you planning to go?"

I haven't decided yet, but I'm only planning a trip within the city," I replied, looking at the spines of the books. Just then, my hand caught something old and dusty. I pulled out that book that resembled a diary.

"I've never seen this book before," Casper remarked.

"It looks like a diary," I said, examining it closely.

"Don't you know it's considered a bad habit to read someone's diary?" he questioned with a raised eyebrow.

"I didn't, but it looks fascinating, and it's in the library; someone must have read it before," I replied.

"Looks like you're really eager to dive into someone's life right now. Alright," Casper said with a smile, extending his hand for a shake.

"Bye, thanks for the book," I said, shaking my hand and turning to leave, heading towards the library doors.

"See you around, Ellie," he replied. It was the first time he had ever called me by my nickname, it was the same nickname my father calls by.

I was returning home from the library, surprised by Casper's unexpectedly sweet behaviour. I was happy until I arrived at the house. The house was shrouded in darkness, and the grey walls were making me sick. I put the book and bag in the bedroom. I craved some ice cream and headed to the kitchen for a cup of ice cream. I noticed my young neighbor was playing with her father through the kitchen window. The sight brought tears to my eyes. My father died last year. He killed himself and brought an end to his life.

I just stormed to my bedroom. I was lying over my bed, tears accompanied me. A battle of rage raged within me. My father was a poet, and he was writing his last poem verse when killed himself. My mother often said I inherited my writing skills from him. I felt an overwhelming wave of sadness. Unable to hold my emotions over me, I let them take over. I cried till I lost my consciousness, feeling the weight of my grief and the echoes of what used to be.

I woke up to realize I had only dozed off. I opened my notes to work on my calculus when I heard a knock on the door.

"Come in," I replied. My mother entered, looking exhausted. Her eyes were red and swollen as if she had been crying for hours. She approached me and hugged me. It was comforting indeed, but I felt odd. Her tears made my shoulder go wet; I didn't dare to ask her what was wrong. She stood there, quietly wiping away her tears.

"Are you studying Calculus?" She asked, her voice trembling.

"Yes, Mother," I replied, trying to focus on my work.

"I will prepare the dinner, will let you know, when I'm done," She said and stormed away.

I watched her go, a feeling of guilt and uncertainty. I could understand my mother's fear; she was terrified of losing me the same way she lost her husband. My father was reading a poetry verse in the final moments of his life. I tried to distract myself with calculus, but my thoughts of him were crawling like a spider. He had always been my supporter, no matter what. I miss him deeply and needed a way to distract my thoughts.

I pulled out my Air Pods and started to play songs.

It's been an hour, and I felt alright, a sense of calm rushed over me. Listening had brought a moment of peace.

"Ellen, dinners on the table," Mother called out. I hurried downstairs to join her. Since my father's passing, Mom held on to the responsibility of taking care of me, while my uncle helped me with the emotional side of things, his role as my therapist.

"Ellen, have you planned your trip?" Mom asked as we ate,

"Well, I'm planning to go to Wooden Cabin," I replied

"The one in the woods?" she asked a hint of nostalgia in her voice.

"Yeah, Mom. I know that place well, so it's both safe and thrilling," I answered.

"I asked professionals to clean the place last week," She said.

"That's nice," I replied

"When were you planning to leave?" She questioned me.

"Tomorrow morning," I replied and continued my dinner.

She didn't say anything more and continued with her meal. After dinner, I did my chores and headed to my room. Conversations between my mom and me are scattered; she's often busy with her schoolwork, and I'm wrapped up with my own work. She cared for me, but it often feels like there's a gap between us.

Lying in my bedroom, I realized the pile of emotions I had experienced today. While looking around my room, I noticed the book I had brought from the library. It looked dusty, so I wiped it with a tissue. It's a leather-covered book, flipping through the pages, I realized they were handwritten. I searched for any information about the book's owner but found none. I was about to read the first page.

"Ellen, time to sleep," My mother shouted while knocking on the door.

I closed the book and tucked it under my bed, hoping my mother wouldn't find it. Then I went to sleep, my mind was filled with curiosity about the book.

3

I woke up early, unable to sleep. The excitement of the trip made me dynamic, so I decided to use the time productively. I began packing my clothes into my bag, carefully arranging each item to ensure everything fit neatly. Among the essentials, I made sure to include the book I had found in the library.

Descending the stairs, I found my mother preoccupied herself with a magazine, the soft rustling of pages, and the comforting aroma of breakfast from the kitchen. She had prepared a spread of my favorite morning foods, which I gratefully sat down to enjoy at the dining table.

"Be careful while going, dear," my mother said, her voice filled with concern.

"Yeah, Mother," I replied, trying to sound reassuring even though I could feel her worry.

As I finished my meal and stood up to leave, my mother reached out, taking my hand in hers. Her hug was a mix of warmth and sadness, a silent expression that she struggled to convey her emotions. I hugged her back, creating a bond of reassurance. I was excited for the journey ahead. With one last glance, I headed out to embark myself on the trip.

I set out for the forest with my backpack, eager for an adventure ahead. The cold breeze brushed against my skin, making it chillier than usual. I continued to walk till I reached the entrance of the forest area.

As I walked into the forest, I suddenly heard rustling behind me. For a moment my heart leapt into my throat, and I turned around, but there was nothing behind me. In the silence, I could hear some rustling of leaves in the breeze.

I kept on walking and could hear some footsteps, prompting me to turn back to the trail.

"Casper," I gasped, taking a step back. He stood in front of me.

"Sorry, Ellie," he said, raising his hands in the air, in mock surrender. "I didn't mean to scare you."

I let out my breath. I hadn't realized I was holding, my heart was still racing. "What are you doing here?"

Casper's tone shifted to something more sincere. "I just wanted to come along with you."

"To come where?" I asked, not hiding the irritation within me.

"I just thought I'd join you as a surprise, not to scare you," he said, sounding genuinely concerned.

I narrowed my eyes, trying to understand his motives. "You could have told me. Instead, you tried to scare me. I thought this was supposed to be a solo trip."

"I'm sorry, but can I join you?" he requested with the eyes of a child.

"Alright," I said, deciding to let it go for now. "Have you been in the woods before?" I asked to make sure it's not his first time.

"Don't worry, It's not my first time," He replied, reassuring me.

"Alright," I said and signaled for him to join me. I couldn't help myself from suspecting unexpected friendly behavior from Casper.

We had been walking for the past 40 minutes, and I realized we hadn't exchanged a single word. I decided to break the silence by saying, "I checked the book you gave to me."

"The one you borrowed from the library?" he asked, his breath coming in short gasps.

"Yeah," I replied, not wanting to make a big deal out of it.

"Did you read it?" he inquired, raising an eyebrow in curiosity.

"Nah, but it turns out to be a collection of short stories rather than a diary," I said.

"Is it? Good for you I guess," he said, his face showing interest.

As we continued walking, we reached a wooden cabin. Casper looked in amazement and asked, "Do you own this place?"

"Technically, my mother owns it," I retorted with a smile.

"I have never been in a wooden cabin before. It's fascinating," he said, sounding like a kid on Christmas morning.

"Let's go inside and make some arrangements for the campfire and stuff," I said with a hint of authority.

I unlocked the door, revealing a cabin that had been cleaned by professionals the previous week. I opened all the windows to let in some fresh air and began placing food supplies in the kitchen. Casper stayed still, observing the paintings on the hallway walls with keen interest. It was clear he was captivated by the art.

I went upstairs to place my backpack and make my bed. On my way back down, I noticed a room opposite mine and decided to prepare it so Casper could stay there. After grabbing the book from my backpack, I returned downstairs and saw Casper lying on the couch in the hallway.

"Ellie, I've got a question for you," he said.

"Yeah? Go for it," I replied as I headed into the kitchen to fetch a glass of water.

"Who painted that painting?" he asked, pointing at one of the artworks.

"It was painted by my father," I said, returning with two glasses of water and handing one to him.

"Your father was interested in art and writing, right?" he questioned me.

"Yeah, Casper," I replied, taking a sip of my water.

"Sure, you must have inherited your writing skills from him," he remarked.

"I might have, but I'm not sure. I don't write like he did, he was quite prodigious," I said about my father.

"I've never read any of his work!" he exclaimed.

"Would you like to have some coffee?" I asked to distract the conversation away from my father.

"Of course!" He was restored.

I went inside the kitchen and started to make coffee, I heard some wood moving sound, I came into the hallway, and found Casper placing his art supplies.

"Is it okay if I repaint your father's work?" He asked me.

"Yeah, alright," I went inside to continue making coffee.

I came out noticing he was trying to paint exactly like my father, I handed him the cup of coffee.

"I guess you tucked yourself into painting?" I questioned,

"This painting is really interesting, I want to recreate it badly," he retorted to me.

I sat on the couch and opened the book, the rustling sound of pages filling the quiet neighborhood as I began to read the first page.

"Humans are the worst and the best creatures in the world. Human life is something you can't trust anyone with. If you trust someone, it's like asking for sunlight in the darkest hour of the night. There is one person who feels like they could bring sunlight into your dark night. Well, it feels amazing at the nick of the point because we humans always get amazed by illusions. Also, it takes ages to realise that it was an illusion rather than reality. We are left to trust no one, and that makes life interesting."

It was quite interesting, I liked the first page and I turned my page, which was titled "Disclaimer."

There's a disclaimer for this book? Interesting it's pulling me to read it. I began to read it:

"This book contains ten stories, each exploring how human behaviour responds to various problems. While problems themselves may not be significant, our reactions to them are crucial. Each story carries its own grief."

That's a rather unusual disclaimer. I was about to turn the page and read what was about to be uncovered, Casper interpreted, "Its sunsetting, continue reading later and set up the campfire before the light fades completely,"

I looked outside; the sky looked amusing "I guess you're right"

"Yeah," he agreed.

4

I placed the book down on the coffee and ventured into the deep forest, searching for firewood. Casper was busy arranging the chairs and laying out food and essentials for the evening.

I chopped wood with an axe and carried the logs back to the campfire site. After some effort, I managed to get the fire going, its warm glow in the encroaching sunset. Casper and I settled down with our Diet Coke, and the sunset unfolded before us in a breathtaking display.

The sky was an explosion of colours, fiery oranges and radiant pinks, which painted the horizon with an almost surreal beauty. The sun hung low, casting a warm, golden light as it set. The fire crackled next to us, its heat a cosy contrast to the cool evening. We sat quietly, enjoying nature's beautiful ending.

I was mesmerised by the sunset in the woods. It had been years since I last visited. I remember coming here with my father when I was little, those were magical times. We'd roast marshmallows together, and those were the sweetest days of my life. Sadly, I've missed those moments with him. But now, I'm lucky enough to witness these sunsets again

"You feel nostalgia within you Ellie?" He inquired.

"Yeah, I used to come here every year with my father, until he passed away," I said, the fact my father is no longer alive, haunts me like a sky filled with storm clouds, mirroring the turmoil within myself.

"Have to read the book?" He asked, trying to distract me, because my face showed discomfort when talking about my father.

"No, I just read the Introduction," I replied.

"Oh, is that true that you liked to read books aloud," He inquired.

I was shocked that he knew I loved to read books out loud and questioned him out of curiosity, "Yeah, how did you know?"

"You've never been spotted at the school library, and people were talking about it," he laughed.

"Oh, is it?" I asked him in surprise.

"Why don't you read this book out loud?" he suggested, handing me the book I had left on the coffee table.

"Oh, should I read?" I asked Casper

"Of course!" He said eagerly.

I pulled the book out slowly, the weight of it feeling almost ritualistic in my hands. Casper watched me with a mix of curiosity and concern, his eyes snapping between me and the book.

I opened the book to where I had left off, my fingers tracing the edges of the handwritten pages, feeling the slight hollow where the pen had pressed into the paper. And then, I started to read.

Chapter 1

The story was about a local apothecary from the 1750s, a woman who suffered from somnambulism, whose life had been marked by both her skill in healing and the dark suspicions that surrounded her.

I inherited my apothecary skills from my mother. She was well-respected for her knowledge of herbs and medicines, but her death remains a mystery. Some say she was killed, others say she jumped from a cliff. No one knew how she died, or no one ever told me? I was filled with thoughts, whirling around me.

Every day, villagers visit me, seeking help for their ailments and remedies for their sorrows. They thanked me for curing their problem, but their smiles were disguised by a fear that ran deep down, in their eyes.

I blame my sleep for everything. It all started that night when I woke up in a different region, covered in mud and dirt, with no memory of how I got there. It felt like someone had dragged me. I was terrified, like my fear was a starless night, where no light of comfort existed.

Villagers claimed I was wandering in the woods in the middle of the night, my eyes open but unseeing, my hands clutching at the air. They said it was beyond reality. Since then, I wake up in different places every day. It never stops. One day, I found myself at the edge of a cliff; another time, in the middle of the woods. Every night, my eyes turn blue, leaving me in confusion. Why am I walking to these places? I'm scared to face people who think I'm possessed by evil spirits.

The villagers' rumours grew louder with each passing night as I continued to walk in strange places. Many claimed I was possessed. I tried to explain that I wasn't, that nothing was wrong with me, but how could I explain something I wasn't even aware of? How could I defend myself when I had no memory of what I had done? The darkness of night engulfed me, like a blackness that swallowed me whole, only to spit me out in places I didn't recognize.

The villagers' fear turned to suspicion. They avoided me in daylight too. No one visited for remedies. I was isolated like a ghost wandering my own home felt like a small island, surrounded by an endless sea of unfamiliar faces and distant voices. I was haunted by the things I couldn't remember, my thoughts torn between reality and death. Everyone was afraid to talk to me, except Mary, the blacksmith's daughter.

"Aren't you scared of me like the others?" I asked her.

"You're human, like me. Why would I be scared of you?" she retorted, smiling. She was young but the sweetest girl, her smile brighter than the sun. She was the one who believed nothing was wrong with me.

I heard people saying I was seen standing in the village square, my hands outstretched towards the sky, my mouth moving in silent prayer. They said I looked like a woman possessed, like a creature of the night. That was the night they declared me a "witch."

I was terrified of myself. Nights became a prison, darkness a place where I no longer had control. I woke up to find scars all over my body, my feet bloodied from walking over sharp stones. I was exhausted, but sleep brought no rest, only more torment. The villagers watched me now, waiting for me to make a mistake, to do something that would confirm their fears. I saw it in their eyes when they passed me on the street, in the way they crossed themselves as if to ward off evil.

I tried to leave the village once, thinking a change of place might free me from this curse. But the nights followed me, and I awoke miles away, standing on the edge of a cliff with the wind howling around me.

I am afraid, afraid of what I might do, afraid of what I might become. I've heard the whispers, the rumours that I'm in league with dark forces. They say I am the cause of the ill fortune that has befallen the village, that my presence is a blight on the land.

The day I feared came on August 14th. I woke with the taste of dirt in my mouth, the smell of damp earth clinging to my skin like a shroud. My clothes were stained with mud and something darker, something I dare not examine too closely.

I don't remember leaving my bed last night. I don't remember walking into the night, but here I am, back in my home with dawn breaking and a feeling of dread so heavy I can hardly breathe. My feet are raw, bleeding from what must have been a long journey over rough ground, yet my mind is a blank canvas, devoid of any image that might explain this horror. Even hell isn't as horrible as what I'm living through now.

I know the villagers have been talking about me, but I don't care about their foolish gossip. I am more afraid of what I might find if I look too closely at myself, at these hands that are no longer my own.

I tried to clean myself, to wash away the filth, but the water did nothing. The stains remained, a sickening reminder that something terrible had happened, something I could not bring myself to fully grasp. They say a child is missing, little Mary, the blacksmith's daughter. I saw her just yesterday, playing in the square with her dolls, her smile as bright as the summer sun. They say she did not return home last night, and that her mother has been searching for her since dusk. I cannot stop shaking.

5

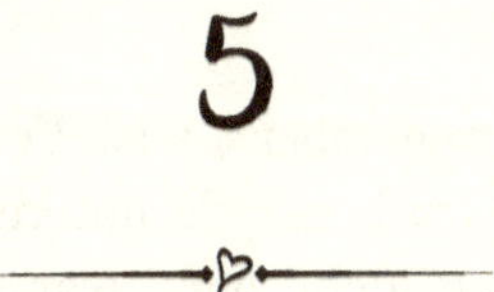

There is a part of me that wants to run, to flee this place and never return. But where would I go? I am bound to this village, to these people who now look at me with suspicion and fear. They do not say it outright, but I see it in their eyes, they think I had something to do with her disappearance.

I don't know what to believe. I cannot remember anything, but there is darkness inside me, a pit that grows deeper with each passing hour. What if they are right? What if I am the monster they fear?

The villagers are gathering outside. I can hear their angry murmurs, and feel the weight of their accusations pressing in on me from every side. I am too afraid to leave, too afraid to stay. I am trapped in this nightmare, unable to wake, unable to escape the horror of what I might have done.

The door is being knocked on now, and I know they are coming for me. I can hear the blacksmith shouting my name, his voice filled with grief that cuts through the fog in my mind.

"You flighty witch, open the door!" someone shouted.

"Where is my daughter, you witch?" Mary's father shouted.

I wish I could remember. I wish I could tell them I am innocent. But the truth is, I do not know. I do not know what happened last night, but I fear that the truth, if it ever comes to light, will destroy me. If I am the one who took her, if I am the reason she is gone, I don't think I can bear to live with myself. The darkness inside me is growing, and I fear it will consume me whole before this day is done. I don't want to be alive anymore, not if this is what I am, not if this is what I have become. They are breaking down the door now. My mind is racing, but there is no time. They will find me soon, and when they do, I know they will not show mercy.

"God help me, I don't know what I've done." I pleaded

They have broken down the door. People are screaming, "Witch!" The blacksmith saw me, his eyes filled with rage. He was surrounded by many villagers.

"Witch!" one of them screamed, and the word caught like wildfire. "Murderer!"

They dragged me from my home, grabbing me by my hair, their hands rough and unforgiving, their rage a living thing that surrounded me, suffocating me. I stumbled and tried to resist, but there were too many, and I was too weak, too afraid.

The square was a mass of bodies, all of them turning to watch as they dragged me into the centre, where the old oak tree stood, its gnarled branches casting long shadows in the early morning light. They shoved me against it, the bark biting into my skin as they forced my arms behind me, tying my wrists with coarse rope. The villagers pressed in closer, a wall of faces filled with hatred and fear.

"Where is she?" the blacksmith demanded, his voice trembling with rage. "Where is my Mary?"

"I don't know," I whispered, tears streaming down my face. "I don't know."

But they didn't believe me. They couldn't. The fear had already taken root, and there was no reason left in them now. They had already made up their mind, I was guilty, and nothing I said could change that.

They decided to kill me by throwing stones. The first stone came from the blacksmith himself, colliding with my cheek so hard I could see my guardian angel. Pain exploded in my head, and I cried out, begging them to spare me. I was screaming for help, pleading for mercy. But no one listened. More stones came, raining down on me with brutal force, each one a punishment for a crime I couldn't remember committing.

"You killed her!" they shouted. "You took her from us!"

"No!" I tried to scream, but my voice was lost in the chaos, drowned out by their fury. My vision blurred, the world collapsing as the beating continued, the pain growing more intense with every passing second. Blood filled my mouth, but there was no escape, no respite. The stones kept coming, a relentless storm of violence that I couldn't withstand. The people I had cared for my whole life were now beating me to death. Indeed, humans are cruel beings. They blame me for something I haven't committed.

I didn't know how long it lasted—minutes, hours—everything blurred together into an endless haze of pain and fear. My strength was fading, my body growing heavier and weaker until I could no longer stand. The ropes bit into my wrists as I sagged against them, my legs too weak to support me any longer.

But they didn't stop. They wouldn't stop until I was dead.

Through the fog of pain, I heard the blacksmith again, his voice cracking with grief as he screamed at me, demanding to know where his daughter was. But I had no answers, only my terror and the growing certainty that this was how I would die alone, beaten, and broken, tied to a tree like an animal. Blood dripped from my nose, mouth, and ears.

And then, amidst the chaos, I saw her.

Mary.

She stood at the edge of the crowd, her small face pale and ghostly, her eyes wide with fear as she watched the violence unfold. She looked so fragile, so lost, and for a moment, our eyes met. Mary, the blacksmith's daughter, was alive.

I tried to call out to her, to tell them she was there, that she was alive, but the words wouldn't come. My throat was too raw, my body too broken. All I could do was watch as she slowly faded from view, her image blurring until she was nothing more than a distant memory, a fleeting ghost in the morning light.

The blows slowed, and then stopped altogether. The crowd fell silent, their breath coming in ragged gasps as they stared at me, their anger replaced by something else, something like fear, or perhaps regret. But it was too late for that. Far too late.

I felt myself slipping away, my consciousness fading, the pain growing distant as the world darkened around me. The last thing I heard was the blacksmith's voice, a broken whisper that echoed in the silence.

"She's gone," he said. "She's really gone."

And then, there was nothing.

Aquilla Ravenswood died that day, beaten to death by the people she had served and tried to heal. They buried her in an unmarked grave at the edge of the village, her name erased from their memory, her story forgotten. But the curse that haunted her family did not die with her. It lived on, buried deep in the roots of the village, waiting for the next soul to stumble upon its darkness.

She was not a curse but a victim of somnambulism. It's impossible to find mercy within when selfishness runs through their veins.

I shut the book immediately.

I was lost in my thoughts; I was adrift in my own sea of confusion and disbelief. My mind felt like an ocean, waves of doubt and anger crashing over me, threatening to pull me under. How could they accuse her of something she didn't do? The injustice of it all weighed heavily on my heart.

"It's better if we head inside the cabin," Casper finally said, breaking the oppressive silence.

"Yeah," I agreed, glancing up at the sky. "The light's already fading."

We made our way back to the cabin, but with every step, my heart pounded harder in my chest, thoughts of the story swirling in my mind like a storm. The first chapter had already sunk its claws into me, and I couldn't shake the image of Aquilla's final moments.

Once inside, we settled into the cabin's dim light, but the unease lingered between us. It felt like an eternity had passed before either of us spoke again, and even then, the words were few, our minds still haunted by the story we had uncovered.

"Aquilla" I finally whispered, my voice barely more than a breath. "She didn't deserve that."

Casper exhaled sharply, a sound somewhere between a sigh. "She didn't even know what she was doing. They... they killed her for something she had no control over." His tone filled with a raw edge of anger and disbelief that echoed the turmoil in my own heart.

"But somnambulism… it's-" I hesitated, the words sticking in my throat. "It's not even something people talk about today. Sleepwalking. It's so… harmless."

"Not back then," Casper muttered, running a hand through his hair, his frustration. "Back then, everything unexplained was a curse, a sign of witchcraft. They didn't care about the truth, Ellie. They just wanted something, someone to blame."

I nodded, feeling the weight of his words settle over me like a shroud. "But how could they? How could they do that to her?"

"They were afraid," Casper said, his voice low as if speaking too loudly might shatter the fragile moment. "Fear makes people do terrible things, Ellie. They didn't understand what was happening, and instead of trying to, they let their fear turn into violence."

"Yeah, Fear makes people do terrible things, that very truth, and even in our own time, there were still echoes of that same fear, that same darkness", I replied, My voice sounded as if I was shattered in pieces by a storm.

"The pain she was going through… it was truly heartbreaking," Casper said, his voice thick with emotion.

"Yeah," I murmured, "sometimes we can't fully grasp the depth of someone else's suffering."

"Conversations about only bringing back the depth of sorrow into our Ellie" He spoke, his voice low as he was completing the sentences.

My mind turned into turmoil. After reading the first chapter in the book, It felt like supporting my essay, Humans indeed are the most cruellest beings ever existed. Imagination of death was horrible, They threw stones and beat her till she left the last breath of her life. The story might be fictional or real, not sure what to trust. It's diving in a storm. People didn't care about her, while she was helping with all kinds of difficulties. She cured many people, But No one thought of mercy. She pleaded with them, begged them to spare. She was punished for something she didn't commit. The daughter of the blacksmith, Mary was Alive.

6

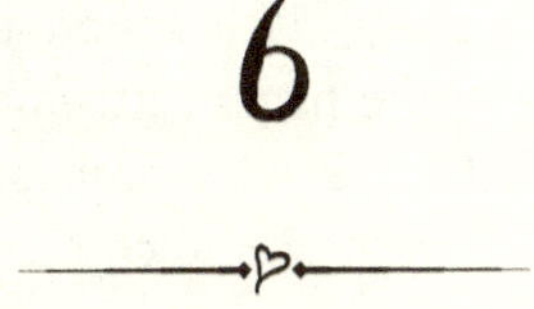

"Ellie", Casper called me out, But my thoughts whirling in my head.

"ELLIE", Casper shouted.

"Yeah", I gasped.

Casper gently took the book from my hands, his eyes filled with concern as he said, "This book is causing turmoil within you, Ellie."

"Maybe," I admitted, my voice trembling between fear and rage. "But the only way I can distract myself is by reading the other chapters."

"Are you sure about your decision, Ellie?" he asked, his gaze steady, searching for reassurance.

"I know these chapters are leaving us with more questions than answers, but this might be the only way to piece together the jigsaw puzzle that's been haunting me," I replied, trying to steady my racing thoughts.

Casper nodded slowly, his expression thoughtful. "Fear can indeed change us, turn us into different beings," he said, almost as if he were talking to himself.

With a deep breath, he opened the book. The rustling of pages filled the room, each sound making my heart pound faster. Finally, the pages settled, and Casper began to read. The air felt thick with anticipation as we both braced ourselves for what was to come.

Chapter 2

Josephine Whitlock, once a vibrant and lively young girl, falls ill with a severe fever that nearly takes her life. Although she physically recovers, it causes her to believe that her body is rotting, that she has no internal organs, and that she is a walking corpse. She suffered from Cotard's delusion

I woke up, drenched with sweat; my skin was burning as if it were on fire. The fever has taken hold of me again. It comes in waves, leaving me weak and trembling. Mother says it will pass, that I must be strong. But I am so tired, so tired that each breath feels like a battle, and my mind is slipping away from me. I fear I am losing myself.

The doctor visited me this morning. He looked at me with pity in his eyes, but his words were of little comfort. He asked to take rest and remedies, suggesting I wait out the fever, but I could see on his face that he was not hopeful. I am not hopeful either. I feel as though something inside me is breaking, something that cannot be mended.

The fever finally broke, but it has left me hollow. My body is still; my thoughts are fighting like women seeking for their rights. Everything feels distant as if I am looking at the world through a fog. The fog engulfed me completely leaving me unable to breathe. I feel nothing, no joy, no pain, just emptiness. I overheard Mother talking to Father; she sounded relieved that I was improving. But I am not improving. Something is terribly wrong. I stare at myself and feel empty. It's like the body doesn't even belong to me. I was pale, looking like a corpse.

"Father, what if I looked different? What if I looked... dead?" I asked, a hollow emptiness settling within me.

"Don't be silly, dear," he replied, chuckling as if I were making a joke. But I wasn't being silly. I knew what I saw, what I felt. Or rather, what I no longer felt.

The darkness inside me is growing. I can feel it spreading, like a rot that is consuming me from within. I looked in the mirror today, and what I saw was not me. It was a ghost, a shell of a person. My skin is grey, my eyes are sunken. I touched my face, but it felt like touching cold, dead flesh. I am dead. I know it. I can feel it in my bones. Maybe this is what they called death. No one believes me. Father thinks I am still recovering, and that I just need time. But time won't fix this. I am beyond fixing. I told Mother that I was dead, but she just cried and told me not to say such things. But how can I not? It is the truth. I am a walking corpse, and no one sees it but me.

I cannot eat anymore. The thoughts of food are making me sick. What's the point of eating, When I'm already dead? I tried to force down some bread this morning, but it turned to ash in my mouth. I spat it out and pushed the plate away. Mother looked at me with worry in her eyes, but I couldn't explain it to her. She wouldn't understand. I avoid mirrors now. I cannot bear to see what I have become. My reflection taunts me, a constant reminder that I no longer belong to this world. I am trapped in this decaying body, a prison of flesh that is rotting from the inside out. The smell of death follows me everywhere. I can't escape it. I am trapped in this nightmare, and there is no waking up. Mother tries to comfort me, but her touch feels like ice. I pull away; telling her not to touch me, that she'll catch whatever it is that I have. But she just cries and tells me I'm not making any sense. Maybe I'm not. But what does it matter? None of this matters anymore.

I don't leave my room anymore. There is no point. The world outside is no longer mine. I belong to the darkness now, to the cold void that has consumed me. I sit by the window and watch the world go by, but it is as if I am watching it from another realm, a place where I do not exist.

Father brought the doctor back again. He asked me questions. He concluded by saying that I am physically healthy and that it is my mind that is unwell. But he is wrong. It is not my mind, it is my body. My dead, rotting body. They all think I'm mad, but I know the truth. I am dead, and I am just waiting for my body to catch up. I tried to explain it to my parents, to make them see what I saw. I told her that I was dead and that I could feel the decay spreading through me, but she just looked at me with tears in her eyes and shook her head. She doesn't understand. None of them do. I am alone in this. They've started to avoid me. Even Father, who used to sit with me every evening, now finds excuses to be elsewhere. I can see the fear in their eyes. They are afraid of me, of what I have become. I don't blame them. I am afraid too.

The silence in the house is deafening. No one talks to me anymore. They pass by my room as if it doesn't exist, as if I don't exist. Maybe I don't. Maybe I am just a ghost, lingering in this world, unable to move on. I feel nothing but emptiness, a void where my soul used to be. I wander through the house at night, unable to sleep, unable to find peace. The darkness is my only companion, the only thing that understands me. I am alone in this house, alone in this world. I am a ghost, a shadow, a dead girl trapped in a body that refuses to die.

The days blend into one another now, a haze of grey mornings and endless, sleepless nights. I no longer feel the passing of time. It's as if I'm suspended in a never-ending Fight, caught between life and death, unable to move forward, unable to go back. The house is quiet, too quiet, and the silence weighs heavily on me, pressing down on my chest until I can barely breathe.

I've tried to explain to Father again, to make him understand that I am no longer alive, but he refuses to listen. He dismisses my words as nonsense and tells me I need to rest, to eat, to try and regain my strength. I am a hollow shell, a corpse animated by some cruel trick of fate. Every time I speak, I see the confusion and fear in his eyes, and it breaks me a little more. He can't see the truth, the horror that I am living.

The villagers avoid our house now. They whisper that I am cursed, that something unnatural has taken hold of me. I hear them sometimes, outside my window, their voices carrying on the wind. They say I am a bad omen, that the fever has stolen my soul and left something else in its place. They are right, in a way. I am not the same person I was before. I don't know who I am anymore, or what I've become. I am so tired. Tired of fighting, tired of trying to convince everyone that I am already dead. They won't listen, no matter how much I beg, no matter how much I cry. They refuse to see what is right in front of them. But I can't give up. I can't keep living, or rather, existing like this. I need it to end. I need to be free of this decaying body, free of this torment.

I've been thinking a lot about death, about what it would be like to truly die. To leave this world behind and find peace, finally, after all this suffering. But I am afraid. Afraid that even in death, I will be trapped in this state, this void between life and death. What if there is no escape?

The only way out, the only way to be sure, is to sever my head from this cursed body. I've read that beheading is the surest way to end a life, to ensure that the soul is released. But how can I ask that of Father? How can I ask him to do something so horrific, something that will haunt him for the rest of his days? And yet, I have no other choice. I cannot do it myself, my hands tremble too much, and my strength is gone.

I don't want to hurt him, but I can't go on like this. I can't bear it anymore. I have to make him understand, somehow, that this is the only way. I have to be free. I have done it. I have asked Father to behead me. The words felt like ash in my mouth, but they had to be said. I could see the horror in his eyes, the way his face went pale as he realised what I was asking. He refused, of course. He said it was madness that I wasn't thinking clearly, that I needed help. But I am thinking clearly. More clearly than I have in months. I know what I am, and I know what must be done.

For days, I begged him and pleaded with him to end my suffering. I told him that this was the only way that I couldn't go on living in this state of undead. He wouldn't listen at first, but I could see the cracks in his resolve and the way his hands shook when he looked at me. He is a good man, my father, and he loves me dearly. But love can be a cruel thing, can't it? It can blind you to the truth, and make you do things you never thought you were capable of.

Finally, after what felt like an eternity, he agreed. The words came out in a whisper, barely audible, but they were there. He said he would do it, that he would end my suffering if that was truly what I wanted. I told him it was. I told him it was the only way to save me.

7

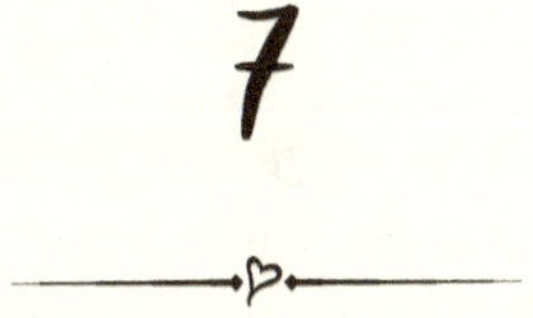

The day has come Aug 14th. I can hardly believe it, even now. Father took me to the clearing in the woods, the one where we used to go for picnics when I was a child. It felt so strange to be there, knowing what was about to happen, knowing that this would be the last place I would ever see. The sun was setting, casting long shadows across the ground, and the air was thick with the scent of pine and earth. It was almost peaceful, in a way.

Father was silent the whole time, his face pale and drawn. He didn't look at me, not once, as he led me to the spot where it would happen. I could see the pain in his eyes, the way he was struggling to keep himself together. It broke my heart, but I couldn't stop now. I had to go through with it. There was no other choice.

He asked me one last time if I was sure if this was truly what I wanted. I nodded, unable to speak. My throat was dry, my heart pounding in my chest. I was terrified, but there was no turning back. I knelt down on the ground, my hands shaking, and closed my eyes. I heard him unsheathe the axe, the sound of the blade cutting through the air as he raised it above his head.

For a moment, everything was still. The world held its breath, waiting for what was to come. And then, with a single, swift motion, it was over.

They found my body in the clearing the next morning. Father had stayed by my side all night, weeping over what he had done. He was the one who told the villagers, who confessed to them that he had taken my life. They say he was out of his mind with grief, that he couldn't bear the weight of what he had done. They say he turned himself in, but no one could bring themselves to console him. How could they? They knew the pain he must have been in, the pain we had both suffered.

Father didn't attend the funeral. They say he's locked himself away in the house that he won't speak to anyone, won't eat or sleep. I fear for him, but there's nothing I can do now. My time in this world is over.

I only hope that, in death, I can find the peace that eluded me in life. That I can finally rest, free from the torment that haunted me for so long.

I am sorry, Father. I am sorry for everything.

"Her father endured the ultimate grief, having to bear the unspeakable burden of beheading his own daughter," Casper said, his voice trembling as his teary eyes sought mine, a storm of rage and anguish battling within himself.

"He couldn't see his daughter suffer in the unbearable pain, He was whirling in emotions that he beheaded his own daughter," I spoke while there was an unbearable rage within me.

"The same daughter, he took care of her from childhood, He couldn't see his daughter suffer and at the same he wished that a day like this never existed in his life," Casper exclaimed.

"I fear the most from me, what if we were dead in some conditions, that was unbearable to accept the truth?" I said while I was floating, a person with extensive thoughts over my mind about the dead.

"We would never know what will happen in future," Casper exclaimed.

"Let's start reading the next chapter?" I insisted on Casper.

Chapter 3

The tale of a young writer suffered from Bipolar disorder,

I'm Jaeson, an outcast author, caught between the stress and the thrill of being alive.

August was an unforgiving month. the air thick with the scent of rain that refused to fall. It clung to the town like a shroud, heavy and suffocating. I watched from my study window as the clouds gathered on the horizon, dark and brooding, just like the thoughts that swirled in my mind. The world outside was a reflection of the storm brewing within me, a storm that had no end in sight.

For days, I had felt it coming, that familiar, dreadful pull. It began as a whisper, a subtle shift in the winds of my mind, stirring up old memories, and old fears. The high was always intoxicating at first, like the rush of a sudden gale that fills your lungs and makes you believe you can fly. I'd ride that wind, reaching for the sun, convinced that I could touch the sky if I just tried hard enough.

But even as I soared, I knew what awaited me when the winds died down.

The crash was inevitable, a fall from grace that left me shattered and broken, lying in the dirt. The world, once vibrant and alive, would turn grey and lifeless. The voices that had spurred me on would twist and warp, becoming mocking echoes that taunted me in my darkest hours.

Today, 14th August, the wind was still high. My thoughts raced faster than I could write them down, ideas bursting forth like lightning in a summer storm. My novel, the one that would finally make sense of everything, was all I could think about. The words flowed from me like a river, untamed and relentless. I couldn't stop, wouldn't stop, because I was certain that if I did, the dam would break and the flood would drown me.

I hadn't eaten in days, hadn't slept, and my body was starting to fail me. But I didn't care. All that mattered was finishing the novel. My fingers ached, the ink smudging on the pages as I scribbled furiously, desperate to capture every thought, every fleeting inspiration before it vanished into the ether.

I knew they were worried like my sister, and my friends. They whispered behind closed doors, their concern for me growing with each passing day. I could see it in their eyes, the way they looked at me like I was a wild animal that might lash out at any moment. But what did they know? They couldn't see the brilliance that was so clear to me. They couldn't understand the urgency, the need to pour out everything inside me before it was too late.

Outside, the sky was darkening, the clouds now a roiling mass of black and grey. I could feel the pressure building, the tension in the air thick enough to cut with a knife. The first drops of rain began to fall, tapping against the window like the ticking of a clock, counting down the moments until the storm would break.

I paused, my hand trembling above the page. The room was stifling, the air too hot, too close. I could feel my heart pounding in my chest, the rhythm erratic, like the beating of a bird's wings trapped in a cage. I needed to breathe, to escape this suffocating place. The walls were closing in, the ceiling pressing down on me, and I knew I had to get out before it crushed me completely.

I stumbled to the door, flinging it open and stepping out into the rain. The cool drops splashed against my skin, a shock to my fevered mind. The world was awash in shades of grey, the colours leached away by the gathering storm. I could see the townspeople hurrying to take cover, their faces blurred by the rain, their voices distant and muted. They didn't notice me standing there, didn't see the turmoil that raged within me. To them, I was just another figure in the downpour, another soul caught in the storm.

But I knew better.

I walked through the streets, the rain soaking through my clothes, each step heavier than the last. The wind howled around me, tearing at my hair, and my clothes as if trying to strip away the last remnants of my sanity. The trees bent and swayed, their branches like skeletal fingers reaching for the sky, begging for mercy that would never come.

I found myself at the edge of town, at the foot of the hill where I had always come to think, to find peace. But there was no peace here today, only the roaring of the storm and the thunder in my veins. I sank to my knees, the earth cold and wet beneath me, and for the first time, I allowed myself to weep. The tears mixed with the rain, indistinguishable from one another, as the storm inside me finally broke.

I knew, at that moment, that I could never finish the novel. It was beyond me, beyond anyone. The brilliance I had chased was nothing more than a mirage, a cruel illusion that had led me to this precipice. I was a fool to think I could harness the storm, could ride it to glory without being consumed by it.

The darkness was closing in, the weight of it pressing down on me, and I was too tired to fight it any longer. I had nothing left to give, no more words, no more ideas. Just the emptiness that had been growing inside me for so long, swallowing everything in its path.

As I lay there, the rain pounding down around me, I thought of the novel, unfinished, like my life. Would they find it, I wondered? Would they read it and understand what had driven me to this? Or would it be lost to time, just another forgotten story, like the countless others buried in the archives of history?

I closed my eyes, the wind howling in my ears, the storm now a distant roar. The rain was a lullaby, soothing in its relentlessness, washing away the last vestiges of my pain. I let myself drift, the darkness pulling me under, and for the first time in what felt like years, I felt at peace.

The storm would pass, as all storms do. The world would go on, unchanged, and uncaring. But for me, the battle was over. I had fought as long as I could, but the storm had won in the end.

As the darkness claimed me, I thought of the novel, the words I would never write, the story I would never tell. And then, there was nothing.

"He was indeed a great poet," I exclaimed, tears welling up in my eyes, as a sudden surge of anger threatened to overwhelm me. Questions about human existence swirled in my mind like a storm. What's the point of life when we don't know what will happen in the very next moment?

Casper slammed the book shut and placed it on the coffee table. He walked over to me, his eyes filled with concern. "What happened, Ellie?"

"When something about poetic death hits me, it feels like my father all over again—he killed himself right in front of me. I had to watch him die, powerless to stop it." My voice cracked as I burst into heavy tears. It was as if a dark cloud had opened up within me, unleashing a downpour of grief. I felt so heavy, like a tree burdened with too much rain, and then I fainted.

After two hours, I found myself on the couch. Casper handed me a cup of coffee as I stirred awake.

"What happened?" I asked, my voice still shaky.

"You fainted. I was worried. What happened? Are you alright now?" His concern was palpable, and for a moment, it felt like I was talking to my father.

"Yeah, I guess I faint when I've had a rough time," I replied, trying to brush it off.

"Oh, is that normal?" he asked, clearly puzzled by my casual response.

"Don't worry, everything's alright," I reassured him.

He let out a sigh of relief and said, "I noticed something strange about the three stories we read."

I can't believe it," Casper, his voice trembling slightly. "All of them... They all ended the same way. August 14th. How is that even possible?"

I shook my head, unable to answer. The sheer horror of the coincidence or perhaps the pattern, was almost too much to bear. "It's as if their lives were predestined to end on that date," I murmured. "But why? What does it mean?"

"Yeah, but we can't be sure if those stories are real," he retorted.

"What do you think the other stories are about?" I asked, my curiosity growing.

"They might have some similarities," he retorted, and the room fell silent.

"Death," I said softly, "seems to be the ultimate escape from the pain they endured. But is it really an escape, or just another form of suffering?"

Casper's eyes were distant as he pondered my question. "Maybe it's both. Maybe they saw death as a release, but it was also a profound end to their struggles. It's hard to imagine what they felt in their final moments, whether they found peace or if it was just another layer of suffering."

We both fell silent again, the weight of our conversation settling heavily on us. It was clear that the stories we had read had affected us deeply, stirring emotions that were difficult to process. The tales of suffering and death had created a bond between us, a shared understanding of the fragility and intensity of human emotions.

"Maybe we should rest," Casper finally suggested, his voice tired. "We need to clear our minds and find some peace before we dive back into this. It's a lot to take in."

I nodded in agreement, though I couldn't shake the unease that had settled over me. "You're right. Let's get some sleep."

We separated each heading to our respective rooms. As I lay in bed, the darkness of the cabin enveloping me, my mind raced with the images and stories we had read.

In the middle of the night, I was awakened by a sudden realisation that the oak tree, the very same tree where Aquilla had been tied and beaten to death, was just behind the cabin, not far from where we were staying.

I considered telling Casper, but the fear of disturbing his already fragile state kept me silent. I couldn't bear the thought of adding to his distress, It was a burden I chose to carry alone, at least for now.

9

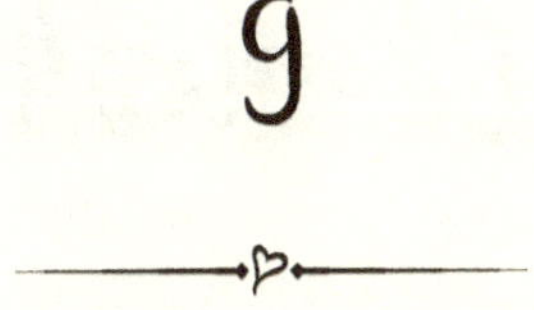

I woke up from my sleep, my mind tangled in the stress of realising that the stories in the book might be true. The weight of that truth bore down on me, like a heavy fog that refused to lift. I found Casper waiting for me in the hallway, holding the book and two cups of coffee. I hadn't mentioned the Aquilla story being true to him, it was too much to process, too heavy to share. Instead, I silently walked over and sank into the couch, the cushions feeling like a temporary refuge.

Casper handed me a cup of coffee, his eyes searching mine for reassurance. "Ellie, it's better if we finish reading the book," he insisted gently.

"Of course, let's start reading," he continued, though I could sense the hesitation in my eyes. My mind wasn't ready for another story of death, but I nodded in agreement anyway, the weight of expectation pulling me along.

Casper opened the book, the pages whispering secrets that neither of us was fully prepared to uncover.

Chapter 4

The story of Marcus and Margaret, where Marcus suffered from Persistent Complex Bereavement Disorder (PCBD), and Margaret promised him that she was willing to die for him, and she proved it one day.

I was waiting for my beloved with a bouquet of lilies in hand. Three hours had passed, but she still hadn't arrived. Just as I was about to turn back, I felt a heavy thud on my shoulder. My face lit up like the bright sun, my heart dancing with joy, much like a child receiving his favourite chocolate. I began to turn around, expecting her.

"Marcus," Evan shouted.

I awoke, realising I had been dreaming. My heart shattered.

"I was dreaming about meeting my beloved Margaret. I guess I wasn't fortunate enough to see her," I said, my heart breaking further with each word.

"It's not all about Margaret, my friend," Evan replied, trying to lighten the mood, but I was lost in thoughts of her.

Margaret was my everything. My life had been engulfed in darkness since my parents gave me up for adoption. I had cried and screamed in those dark rooms, but no one heard my pleas. It felt like I was drowning in the middle of the sea, where not even the waves could carry my voice. The sea heard me every day but stood still, helpless. Then Margaret entered my life; she was the moon to my dark sky, the lifeboat that rescued me. My life shone brighter than the sun with her in it. It was as if rainbows had filled my sky after a torrential storm.

I couldn't digest the fact that I had to live without her. The rage within me stirred a storm, and tears welled up in my eyes. I stared at the floor, tears falling like blood from my heart. My friend Evan tried to console me, but he didn't realise he was trying to treat a man whose heart had stopped beating. Margaret was my heartbeat, and the moment she was buried, nothing felt real anymore. I had lost the purpose of staying alive.

"There might be a world war within months," Evan said, trying to distract me from my grief and break the silence between us.

"Nothing matters to me anymore, Evan. I've already lost the purpose to stay alive," I said, preparing to leave.

"I hope you get better soon," Evan replied, then left the place immediately.

I grabbed Margaret's memories from the shelf and cried. It had been three whole weeks since my beloved left this world. She was the shining moon on my darkest nights, but she had been swallowed by an eclipse. I was weak and trembling, knowing she died in protest. I always regretted not stopping her that day.

I tucked myself in warm clothes, left for the market, and bought a bouquet of lilies. The flowers were fresh and beautiful, just like my beloved's eyes—those eyes I used to gaze into every day. I took the bouquet and went straight to the graveyard.

Margaret.

I found my beloved's grave and placed the lilies on her gravestone. I sat beside it and opened my diary, the pages filled with memories of our time together. I started to read one.

"The very first time I saw Margaret was at a Yule Ball. She wore a shining blue dress that felt like the ocean filled with glitter. She was brighter than any star as if she owned the colour blue. Her dark green eyes, under the light of the candle chandelier, made her look like a star. My heart fluttered at her presence, and I was entirely smitten. My ears turned red, as they always did when I blushed. Margaret never missed an opportunity to tease me about that—she was the first to notice my ears turning red.

Margaret was ready to sacrifice her entire life just to be with me. She left her parents, brothers, and the comfort of her mansion to live with a hopeless activist orphan. I always asked her if she wanted to return to her family, but she would always say she was grateful that I was her family.

On our wedding day, I took vows to protect her until my last breath, but I couldn't save her from dying. I couldn't even attend her cremation. Her parents blamed me, saying I could have stopped her from attending the protest where she died. My tears resembled rain in a silent ocean.

I felt useless. My life was once again filled with gloomy rains. It started to pour, and I was drenched entirely, my clothes soaked through. I didn't move from the spot. I felt a heavy thud in my body and lost consciousness. When I opened my eyes, I found myself in a hospital, accompanied by my friend Evan.

'Have you lost your mind?! You could have died, you idiot. Do you even care about your life?! What the hell is wrong with you, Marcus?!' Evan shouted. I understood his rage—I was fully aware that I could have died. It may seem childish, but deep down, I wanted to die and be with my beloved forever.

'You're seeing a doctor now,' Evan retorted and stormed away.

My thoughts were whirling in my mind. Someone came to visit me, wearing a white coat—he must have been the doctor. He sat in the chair next to me.

'How are you doing, Marcus?' he asked.

'Nothing feels real, not since the moment my beloved passed away,' I replied. He seemed like he wanted to say something, but I interrupted him, requesting to continue the session later. Then, I left the hospital.

I returned home. Every day, I used to hear my wife's voice, but now she is gone. I slept to escape reality. I dreamt I was waiting for Margaret with lily flowers. She was wearing our wedding dress, glowing like an angel."

"Marcus...
We will be united soon. You know what to do," she said to me as she disappeared.

"Yeah, dear, I'll reach you soon..." I replied.

The next day, August 14th, I woke up and cleaned the house. I put on my wedding suit—the suit my beloved Margaret had adored. Then I hanged myself with a rope in the hallway.

Evan knocked on the door, worried when I didn't answer. After breaking it down, he found me hanging from the ceiling. Overcome with shock and trembling, he collapsed to the ground. Evan r found the note I had left for him:

"Oh, my friend. I know you weren't happy with my decision. I've been sulking in this four-walled house for days, living in memory of Margaret. I'm grateful that I will soon be with my beloved. I'm thankful to have you as a friend who supported me until the end of my life. I have one request: can you bury my body next to my wife's gravestone?"

Following Marcus's request, his body was laid to rest next to his wife's grave.

10

The room was steeped in an almost oppressive silence. As Casper finished reading, he closed the book and looked up.

"What are emotions?" Casper asked me.

"People say emotions are feelings," I began, my voice faltering slightly. "I think they're like how eyes can communicate without words and the heart can understand without explanation. Emotions make us human, encompassing both happiness and sadness. They're more than just hormones. I believe emotions are what distinguish living beings from non-living things." My words felt heavy as they caught in my throat.

"Marcus and Margaret, I feel like we've known them for ages," he said thoughtfully. His voice echoed in the quiet space, making my heart race. I had wanted to tell him that every story in this book was real, that the couple Marcus and Margaret were buried beside my father. My hands trembled, and my voice wavered as I tried to find the courage to speak.

"Casper, I need to tell you something," I said, struggling to keep my voice steady. My eyes darted around the room, unable to meet his gaze.

"What is it?" he asked, a note of concern in his voice.

"The oak tree... it's the same tree behind the woods," I continued, my voice breaking as the weight of my words settled like a heavy stone in my chest. "Every story in this book is a real incident." " I asked, trying to keep the fear out of my voice. Casper nodded, his expression growing more serious.

Casper's eyes widened in shock. "Might be!" he said, his voice barely above a whisper.

"Yes," I confirmed, my voice trembling.

Casper took a deep breath, then pulled the book towards him. He closed it with deliberate care, his face a mixture of disbelief and determination. "Let's finish reading the book," he said firmly, his voice resolute despite the fear I could sense underlying his words.

With a sense of foreboding, I watched as he opened the book to the page we had left off. My heart pounded harder with each turn of the pages, the silence of the room now thick with anticipation and dread.

Chapter 5

The Story of Thomas Harrington. He suffered from Post-Traumatic Stress Disorder (PTSD). Thomas was a soldier in World War II.

I was a young seventeen year old standing in the middle of fields, surrounded by flowers and writing songs. I always dreamt of being a singer, I wanted to buy a guitar for myself. My father told me that guitar isn't my forte, I should be going to war and helping our country.

I was forced to be sent as a soldier on the battlefield. Battlefields were not only about winning and losing, but also filled with most disturbing incidents. I was standing in the middle of the battlefield, surrounded by dead bodies around me and scars over my body, holding a rifle. I should still, when vultures are eating my friends alive. I was shooting all the people in my way.

Yeah, I shot many people, Now I'm a MURDERER. The blood splattered all over me. The stain may have washed away from the cloth, but not from my mind. Every night till I was sent home from the war, I can see the people

I killed in my dreams. They were haunting me. I was helpless, My mind felt heavy. They say it's really hard to save a life, but I killed many without mercy. I'm no longer a human, I'm a monster. I was screaming for mercy from the people I killed. I can hear their words saying that I'm a monster.

I had to watch many people die, I was so selfish, only thinking about myself all the time. I planned to escape from the battlefield but I failed. Everyday was turning worse like me into a weaker person. I think hell is far better than living in this rotten world filled with vultures disguised as humans. The crocodile cried when someone died. Those screams for help are haunting me everyday.

I promised many to protect them no matter what, but I ended up the one hurting them. I witnessed mercy killing, rapes, and many sopken incidents over my journey in the war. The world is rotten, I was just a kid, seventeen years old, I didn't mean to suffer. I was screaming to kill me, but ended up surviving till last.

The darkness flowing within scaring every part of me. The river of purity was filled impure by the blood of innocents. Everyday I witnessed hundreds of men die. I tried to protect myself, but I couldn't save anyone.

The weight of the words from people about dying are heavier than the burden of the rifle I was holding. I sit near the dim light of a flickering lamp, thinking the thoughts of my young me thinking that participating in the war would give me the money to buy a guitar. But now the shadows on the walls are haunting me to death.

Once the war had completely ended I was asked to go home. What is the point of winning the war after all it's about death? I walk home through passing streams of water filled with human flesh. I didn't know what to fight for. Is it a war about freedom? Who is having this freedom, when everyone who needs it died in the war? I was holding the body of my friend in the middle of the war. Who will tell his unborn child about his father? I was an entire mess when I reached home. I wanted to talk to someone, what should I say? Whom should I talk to? I want to die rather than live in this place filled with a rotten human race.

14th August, Today, the pain was almost too much to bear. I walked through the fields. Once I used to write songs, the fields were alive and quiet and peaceful just like before. The only thing rotten here was me. The stillness is a cruel reminder of the chaos that I reigned in.

I tried to find solace in simple writing of mine, my letters to my beloved and distant laughter of the children, but even these small comforts are tainted by the shadows of what I 've seen. Each day was a battle, not against the enemy, but against our own mind. I feel like a stranger in my own skin, lost in a world that no longer makes sense.

I am haunted by the faces of those I could not save, by the moments when I hesitated, by the decisions that led to death and destruction. The burden of those memories is chain around my neck, pulling me down into a darkness I fear I will never escape.

I was forced to see a doctor. The doctor says it's PTSD, that it's a condition of the mind, but How do I heal from the war inside my own head? How do I find peace when every working moment is a reminder of the horrors I endured? I wish I could understand, but the more I try to understand myself, the more I feel myself slipping away.

I'm tired, so freaking tired. The weight of my past and the darkness of my present are too much to bear. I'm afraid that I'm reaching the end of my strength fighting against me. The cost of war was of the souls it claimed, even after the fighting had stopped.

I was silenced by the cost of the war, and those suffering of mine I bore remained unknown. I walked near to the river by my house.

I took out my notepad and started to write, hoping my parents would find it near my dead body

"I was holding a gun with pride,
And thinking I will be a guitarist in the war.

I was holding a gun with pride,
and was killing my opponents in the war.

I was holding a gun with pride,
and killed my friends in the war.

I was holding a gun with pride,
and killed many students who were of the age of my children in the war.

I was holding a gun with pride,
and killed my family in the war.

I was holding a gun with pride,
and carrying the dead bodies of my beloved ones in the war.

I was holding a gun with pride,
and started to cry about losing everyone in the war.

I was holding a gun with pride,
and shot myself with the same gun in the war."

And I drowned myself in the waters.

Casper shuts the book, while tears are flowing from his eyes. "He wasn't ready to witness the shroud of darkness."

I was staring at the floor, while my vision blurred, "He just wanted to be a musician. He didn't deserve the pain that made him kill himself."

Casper spoke with a broken voice, I questioned, "Did they deserve the pain and suffering they went through?"

"He was indeed carrying a war inside him, even when he was not on the battlefield," I stated, my words echoing in the room.

"He didn't deserve the haunted nights, as if darkness sought him out as prey," Casper said, his voice so low it was barely audible, creating a pile of emotions within him.

"It makes me think about how we often overlook the struggles of others, especially those who've faced such trauma. We see the heroes, but we don't always see the cost. It's important to remember that there's a human price to everything," I added, while my eyes battled rage and tears.

"He just wanted to be a musician," He cried.

"Do you want to read the next chapter, Casper?" I asked, even my voice was trembling.

"I just need some time to clear my head," I said, getting up from my seat and heading to my room.

As soon as I entered, a wave of heaviness washed over me. Without hesitation, I grabbed my phone and began writing the story for the competition, pouring my emotions into every word. It was a struggle, but as I wrote, I felt a sense of relief slowly settling in.

After finishing, I submitted the story for the competition. I went downstairs, feeling more at ease.

"Feeling better?" he asked concern evident in his voice.

"Yeah, I can distract myself from the thought of Thomas at least," He retorted. And opened the pages he left.

My heart tells me that the chapter we will uncover will show me a bitter truth.

Chapter 6

The Story of Lillian Carter. She suffered from Substance Use depression. Lillian was an activist in the years following World War II.

I've been fighting for so long, for justice, for equality, for those whose voices are silenced by the powers that be. I started everyday protests for justice, many inspired me all my way long. But no one ever tells me how lonely this road is. A road filled with betrayal.

Sometimes, after a long day of protests and speeches, I come home to this empty apartment, and the silence is deafening. I reach for the bottle. It dulls the ache, numbs the pain that gnaws at me from the inside. It left like a way to escape reality. I can't seem to change, but I don't know how to stop it.

I have been addicted to drinking, like a vicious cycle, one I can't break free from. I make these protests anonymous. The government doesn't take kindly to people like me, people who stir the pot, who speak out against the injustices they'd rather keep hidden. They called me a threat, a danger to society. But the real danger is the silence they impose, the way they crush dissent beneath the weight of their authority.

I was protesting everyday, for there was a great future. But who deserves this secured life? When the people I'm trusting are betraying me everyday, I was hiding myself from people, So I won't get caught by the government. They declared a reward for finding me. Everyone turned into cunning wolves. I was caught by the government.

I'm rotting in jail, day by day. They think they've broken me, but the truth is I've been breaking for a long time, piece by piece, soul by soul. Alcohol is the only comfort now, the only thing that keeps the darkness at bay. But even that is starting to lose its hold.

I was slipping myself into a dangerous darkness pit, I'm sure I can't climb out of it. And I'm so tired of fighting, I am pretending that I'm strong enough to withstand this. I'm not. I never was. I'm just a little innocent girl living in the disguise of a strong woman.

It's been months since I've seen the outside world. The guards don't even look at me anymore, like I'm already dead to them. Maybe I am. Maybe I've been dead for a long time, and this body is just a shell, going through the motions of a life that no longer holds any meaning. I don't get food to eat, only a bottle of alcohol with extra intoxicated mixed within.

It feels alive when I drink my alcohol. It blurs the edges of my reality, makes the pain a little less, I was suffering. My drink started to give me more inebriety. I wake from my deep to realise my whole body was beaten or something is happening to me.

They've taken everything from me, Like my freedom, my dignity, my hope. What's left? What's the point of carrying on when all I see ahead is more suffering, more of an endless pain, an unbearable darkness.

I body was entirely exhausted by tortures they have done to me, while I was intoxicated entirely. I've thought about it before, ending it all. But I always stopped myself, told myself I had more to do, that the fight wasn't over yet. But now... It's entirely pointless, I don't even have enough strength. The drink was way more intoxicated than usual. The only thing I was alive for was alcohol.

I've made up my mind. There's nothing left for me here, nothing left to fight for. Maybe in death, I'll find the peace that's eluded me for so long. Maybe in death, I'll finally be free.

14th august, This will be my last entry. By the time anyone reads these words, I'll be gone. I don't want pity, and I don't want anyone to try and understand why I'm doing this. It's not about giving up, it's about choosing my own end, on my own terms.

I've spent my life fighting battles I couldn't win, against enemies too powerful to defeat. I've watched the world crush the spirits of those I love, and I've watched it crush my own. The alcohol was my escape, but even that has turned against me, dragging me deeper into the abyss.

I'm tired. I'm so tired. Of the pain, of the struggle, of the never-ending fight that's consumed my life. I just want it to end.

To whoever finds this, I hope you understand that this was my choice. It was the only choice I had left. Maybe in the end, that's all we really have—the power to choose our own fate.

I broke the alcohol bottle and picked up the shattered piece and cut my wrist multiple times.

Goodbye.

"She was being tortured in many unknown ways in the prison," My heart raced while my voice was trembling.

"Those days were a true horror to live in, don't you think?" Casper looked up to me.

"I think those days were possibly worse than any hell!" I exclaimed.

"Imagine, Many people like Lillian faced those rotten prisons," Casper spoke with the most I ever heard.

"The fact that she was tortured in unbearable ways," I said, a worse feeling of fear I felt unbearable.

"She was abused in ways we wouldn't imagine," He tried to state.

My heart leapt into my throat, I was exhausted by my thoughts and sufferings they faced. My hands were entirely trembling, The tears were dripping from my eyes, like a gloomy rain in the silent ocean. Seeking for justice and truth isn't fair these days? How many could have died in the same way Lillian died. The pain and grief they suffered in their life. It worsened when she was intoxicated and her body had to face unbearable pain, every moment. I fear to be alive after reading her story.

"Do you think the eternal peace of humans is death?" Casper asked me, his voice trembling with the weight of the question.

I looked up from the floor, "It's a profound thought," I said slowly. "Some believed that death is the ultimate solution, a way to find peace from the struggles we face in our life like their sense of purpose seemed lost among the countless stars, swallowed by the vast expanse of uncertainty. But others see it as just another beginning like Even in the midst of their hopelessness, a tiny, steadfast star in her heart offered guidance through the night.

He stared at the floor, "It's hard to believe that death could be peaceful when I think about everything we've faced. The pain, the loss, how can any of that lead to peace?"

I shifted, my expression thoughtful. "Maybe peace isn't about escaping pain but understanding it, finding a way to come to terms with it. Death might be a way to find that understanding, to release from the burdens we carry."

"But what if understanding doesn't come? What if death is just a void, an endless emptiness where we never find peace or answers?" His expressions were like a chaotic storm.

I sighed, clearly feeling the weight of the conversation, "None of us can truly know what awaits us. All we can do is try to make sense of our lives and our struggles while we're here."

"Yeah, even the fact that I'm dead already right?" Casper exclaimed.

"Did you forget, that I'm dead already, I'm just an imagination of yours," He exclaimed with a hectic laugh.

It's true Casper is no longer alive, He was just my imagination," I spoke while staring at the ceiling. While my heart started to race to face the fact.

12

"The fact was that I was the one imagining Casper was alive these all days, he was just my imagination, I tried to push away, but he was like veil covered my entire thoughts," I signed

Casper died in a car accident last year. He was the only friend of mine. He was the one who used to talk to me, But his death has created a void of darkness around me. I wasn't ready to accept his death. It felt like we were oceans apart.

People say that our minds are creative and beyond our expectations. It always makes us feel comfortable even when we had a rough time within ourselves like a small boat caught in a raging storm, tossed around by engulfing waves. Casper was like a mirage in the desert, glimmering just beyond reach.

My mother insisted I go to therapy the very next moment I could see Casper. I know she was afraid of my well-being, but it feels like home. I am comforted by his presence around me, even It's all my illusion.

This world indeed was rotten to death, No one cared about others, we were only people to our selfishness, we rub off our desires on others.

"Aren't you tired?" Casper asked.

"Yeah, I'm tired actually," I yawned.

"Even the light is fading, why don't you sleep?" He told him.

I realised I was hooked on the book in the morning, and had not felt hungry at all. I was surprised by my state. I don't have any appetite. So I went to sleep.

The next morning I woke up making myself some pancakes. I felt alive for a moment.

"Will you start reading the book?" He questioned me.

"Yeah," I retorted. I picked the book from the bedroom. And opened the book. With a sign, I turned pages to read the very next chapter.

Chapter 7

The Story of Dr. Jonathan Hale, who suffered from Alien hand syndrome. His syndrome brought him a misluck, which made the darkness engulfed with him.

I was a well known heart surgeon in the city. I was driving home one night, and I met with a terrible accident. I woke up from a coma after 4 weeks. My parents were worried about me. I was reassured that nothing had happened to me, but the doctor who treated me wanted to talk to me in person.

I was sitting still, He started to say, "I'm sorry sir, But you were diagnosed with Alien hand syndrome."

I laughed at this statement, "Stopping trying to make fun of it doctor," I replied.

But his facial expressions I could tell that He was serious regarding the Alien hand syndrome. He started to speak , "You're right will no longer be in your control, it might affect the surgeries you will perform. So it's better you retire, sir."

"You remember, you are a younger surgeon, You don't have to advise me what to do!" I replied to him and stormed away.

Next day I woke preparing myself for the surgery I needed to perform.

I drove to the hospital and got dressed and went inside the operation theatre.

I was doing the operation with seriousness in my mind, The operation was about to end. It happened again today. My right hand, the one I've always trusted to save lives, betrayed me in the most grotesque way. I was in the middle of surgery, performing a routine appendectomy, when it suddenly moved on its own. I watched in horror as it sliced too deep, too fast, severing an artery. I tried to regain control, but it was as if my hand had a mind of its own. The patient—God, the patient—I couldn't stop the bleeding in time. She died on the table, and there was nothing I could do.

The others in the operating room looked at me with a mix of confusion and fear, but I couldn't explain it. How could I? How do you tell someone that your own hand defied you, that it acted of its own volition?

I don't know what's happening to me, but it's terrifying. My hand—it's like it belongs to someone else. It does things I don't want it to do, moves when I don't want it to move. I've heard of Alien Hand Syndrome before, but I never thought it could happen to me. Now I'm not sure if I'm losing my mind or if my body is rebelling against me.

I can't sleep. Every time I close my eyes, I see her face—the patient I lost. I hear the monitors' flat lining, the panic in the room. And my hand, covered in blood, moving as if it had a will of its own. I've been trying to control it, to keep it in check, but it's getting worse. It's as if the hand knows I'm afraid of it, and it's feeding off my fear.

I can't let anyone know. If they find out, I'll lose everything—my practice, my reputation, my life's work. But I don't know how much longer I can hide it. Every day is a battle, every surgery a nightmare waiting to happen. And the guilt—it's unbearable. I killed her. My hand killed her, and I'm the one who has to live with it.

I've been drinking more, trying to numb the pain, trying to forget. But nothing helps. The hand is always there, waiting for me to slip up, waiting for another chance to destroy everything.

It's getting worse. The hand is more active now, more aggressive. It grabs things on its own, slams doors, and even struck a nurse yesterday. I played it off as an accident, but I could see the suspicion in her eyes. They're starting to notice that something's wrong, and it's only a matter of time before they figure it out.

I can't keep doing this. I can't keep putting lives at risk. But what choice do I have? This is all I know, all I've ever wanted to do. But I'm afraid—afraid of what my own body might do, afraid of what I might do.

I tried to talk to a colleague today, to get some advice without revealing too much. But the words caught in my throat. How do you tell someone that you're afraid of your own hand? That you're not in control of your own body?

The only time I feel safe is when I'm alone, with my hand tied down. But I can't live like this. I don't know how much longer I can take it.

Another patient died today. It wasn't during surgery this time—thank God for that—but it was my fault all the same. My hand knocked over a tray of instruments, and one of them pierced the patient's side. It was an accident, but I know the truth. It was my hand, my cursed hand, that did it.

I'm a danger to everyone around me. I can't trust myself, and no one else can either. I've been avoiding surgery as much as I can, but I can't avoid it forever. Eventually, someone's going to ask questions. Eventually, someone's going to figure out what's wrong with me.

I don't know what to do. I'm trapped in this nightmare, and there's no way out. The grief is suffocating, the guilt is crushing. I'm haunted by the faces of the patients I've lost, by the blood on my hands. My hands. The hand.

I'm losing myself. I don't know how much longer I can keep going like this.

14th August , This will be my last entry. By the time anyone reads this, it will be over. I can't live like this anymore, can't live with the guilt, the fear, the constant battle against my own body. I've lost control, and I can't keep pretending that everything's okay.

I'm doing this to protect others, to make sure no one else suffers because of me. I'm doing this to escape the hell that my life has become. It's not an easy decision, but it's the only one I have left.

To anyone who finds this—please understand that I didn't want this. I didn't want to hurt anyone. I just wanted to help, to heal. But somewhere along the way, I lost myself, and I couldn't find my way back.

I'm sorry.

"He was indeed haunted by the patients who died in his surgery, He was able to save them." I said

"What if could take an early retirement, when he got to know about the Alien Hand Syndrome." Casper said Because he actually made sense.

"A doctor takes an oath to save his patients, but what happens when they die because of his negligence? That haunted him night after night," I said quietly.

"Why do our minds and lives play tricks on us?" he asked.

"We'll never truly understand how life unfolds," I replied, feeling resigned.

"What makes you think that way?" Casper questioned, his tone curious.

"What if I told you I might die the day after tomorrow?" I said, a hint of uncertainty in my voice.

"You've lost your mind," he responded, his expression shifting to something sadder.

13

"Should I read the next chapter?" I questioned.

"Yeah," Casper replied.

I turned to the next page and reading the rustling of pages made a feeling of comfort within me.

Chapter 8

The Story of Beatrice Caldwell. She suffered from Capgras syndrome. Beatrice was none other than Ellen Brown's martial grandmother.

My heart raced as I read the first line of the chapter. It's the story of my grandmother. There was an unpleasant feeling taking over me. As I turned the pages.

Today, I had another visit with Dr. Alcott, but something felt off about him. Usually, His dressing sense, the way he spoke with me, It felt like it wasn't Dr. Alcott. I knew him for years, but this man... this imposter... There was something cold, calculating about him. I tried to bring it up, to ask him why he seemed different, but he brushed me off, said I was imagining things. But I'm not. I know what I witnessed.

He thought I'm losing my mind, but I know the truth. Someone has taken Dr. Alcott's place, and trying to deceive me. But I won't be fooled. I have to be careful now, very careful. I can't trust anyone, not even my own doctor.

He came everyday pretending nice like Dr. Alcott. I can see it in his eyes that he was hiding something. I don't know what he wants. He asked about my health, but I could tell that he wasn't really interested. He was probing, trying to get information out of me.

I need to be cautious, especially with the will. I can't let them find it. They'll take everything if they do. I've been thinking about a safe place, somewhere one would think to look. The wooden cabin has many hidden spots, perhaps one of those would be best.

I have to protect everything for my daughter, Marie. Everything in my life was about her.

This imposter is visiting me everyday. He kept asking about my estate, about my finances. I played along, and didn't reveal about one. I can see down his deep soul, he was craving for my fortune, I'm sure of it.

It's no longer safe to keep the will where it is. I've decided to hide it in the old store room hidden in the closet of the bedroom. I'm afraid that this imposter might kill me one day.

I refused to take his medicines, He forced me to take one, I'm strong over my decision. I was living alone in the mansion, anytime this imposter could come in and steal my fortune. I have increased security all over the mansion.

I asked the doctor to not visit me, I'm scared what if I wasn't able to save my own daughter from these cunning wolves. I made sure all my letters about How much I love her were stored in the closet's hidden room in the wooden cabin.

My health worsened, as there were no doctors to treat me. The nights were scaring me alive, I have a constant feeling that someone is watching me. I feel the presence of Dr. Alcott.

My daughter visited me on 14th August, I'm glad she visited me. I was happy to see her. I want to walk like a child towards her with enthusiasm but my health is worse than I expected.

"Mother, why aren't you allowing the doctor to check on you?" she questioned.

I felt alive to listen to my daughter's voice "Dear, Dr. Alcott was replaced by someone trying to steal our fortune."

"You are losing yourself, Are you trying to die?" she shouted at me.

The moment I reliased that she wasn't my daughter, she was replaced by some imposter. I just wanted to meet my daughter.

"I wanted to meet my daughter," I screamed.

"I'm your daughter, mother!" The imposter told.

I took the knife beside me and threatened her to bring back my daughter. I tried to kill the imposter. But instead she killed me that day.

I threw the book away after I read it. I was terrified after reading that my mother killed her mom. I was terrified. I was living with a murderer. I was terrified. I'm scared to death. I felt a thug in my heart, I didn't know what was going wrong with me. I was crying and angry at the same time. I collapsed to the floor. I don't know what was happening to me. I fainted.

After some time, I woke up to realise I had a mild Panic attack.

I went running upstairs to find those letters which my grandmother left for my mother. I opened the closet searching for any door impressions, and found a little opening. I opened it, pulled the old chest out of it. I found many letters and notes in it.

I started to read some:

"Dear Marie,

My love, I know you weren't happy that I didn't agree for your marriage. But I still love you dear. Hope one day I can meet my granddaughter."

I read another one

"Dear Marie,

My love, It's your birthday, usually, Me and you used to celebrate your birthday by throwing a huge party in the mansion. But after You left the house, It was all this old soul wandering around the house like a ghost. I just wanted to talk to you before I die."

There's one more

"Dear Marie,

My sweetheart, My Dr. Alcott was replaced by someone. He is in the disguise of my doctor. I felt scared. I hope you will visit me soon. I'm afraid to be alone in this mansion."

Tears were dripping from my eyes, while I was reading these. I took all those letters and notes and went downstairs and made a post with the address written on my mother's house address and the address was unwritten.

"What are you trying to make out of it?" Casper questioned me.

"I will send these letters and notes to my mother anonymously." I was restored.

"But, why?" he questioned.

"All these, she had the grief of killing my grandmother, unintentionally. At Least she will be free by reading how her mother cared about her," I retired and went to the post box.

After travelling for a while, I finally posted it.

I reached back to the wooden cabin.

14

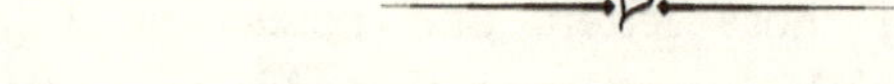

"How do you feel about submitting those letters, Ellen?" Casper asked.

"I feel a bit relieved," I replied. "Knowing that my mother was loved by my grandmother helps more than just stressing over her death."

"We've read through eight chapters already. I'm curious about what's in the ninth one."

"Me too," I said, picking up the book and settling onto the couch.

I opened it to where I had left off and began to read.

Chapter 9

The Story of Victor Brown, A great prodigious poet, who suffered from Paranoid Schizophrenia, The man who never felt to ask the help of others, even he was threw into a dark pit, where light is afraid to reach him.

I gasped when I reliased that the 9th chapter was about my father. I was worried, the curiosity within me, asked to read it completely.

The world is a shattered mirror reflecting a thousand distorted images. I can longer trust my eyes, my ears, my thoughts. There is fine line between reality and illusion, but the line is slipping away. The distorted shadows luking just beyond the edge of my vision, waiting for the moment when I let my guard down.

It wasn't always like this. I remember a time when my mind was a garden of words, blooming verses that spoke of love, loss, and of the world around me. Poetry was my refuge. But now, words turned against me, It's like the voices I hear in my minds were writing from verses. I dismissed them at first, thinking they were just echos of my thoughts, the remnants of dreams that lingered after I awoke. But they grew louder and louder as passes pass.

I could hear them, even as I write this, they slowly whisper my name in my hears giving a chill to my spine. They tell me I'm being watched, that they're coming for me. They say I've been betrayed, that the people I love, My wife and my daughter. I know it's not true. I know these thoughts are a sickness, through my mind. But knowing doesn't help. The fear is too real, too overwhelming. I can't shake the feeling that something is terribly wrong.

My own poetry has become a battleground, a place where i fight a war aganist my own demons in my mind. The vereses I write were twisted dark, filled with many disturbing violence and death. I write about the walls closing in about the feeling of being hunted, about the terror that never leaves.

I got diagnosed, I came to concern, I suffered from Paranoid Schizophrenia, Every day felt like I was kept in a closed dark prison, where lightness feared to enter the prison. I am so scared, I didn't move out of the home. My Wife and daughter were scared about my issues, I didn't tell them the truth. It felt safe in the home, where I can control what comes in and out.

But even here, I'm not safe, The voices follow me, whispering through the walls through the floorboards, through the very thin air I breath. They taunt me, telling me. I'll never escape, that they're always watching, always waiting.

But it's all for nothing. The voices laugh at my efforts, mocking my desperation. They know I'm alone, trapped in this nightmare with no way out. They know I'm on the edge, on the brink of madness.

My poetry has become my only companion, the only voice that doesn't lie to me. But even it has changed, twisted by the darkness that's taken root in my mind. The verses are no longer about beauty or love—they're about fear, pain, and death.

The words flow from me like blood from an open wound, staining the pages with my despair. But they offer no comfort, no release. They only serve to remind me of the darkness that's consuming me, of the madness that's overtaking my mind.

I can't escape it. I can't run from it. It's inside me, a part of me, and it's eating me alive.

The war in my mind rages on, and I'm losing ground. The voices are louder now, more insistent. They tell me I'm being watched, that I'm being followed, that they're coming for me. They say I can't trust anyone, not even my own family.

I've pushed them all away—my wife, my daughter, everyone. I can't bear to see the fear in their eyes, the confusion, the pity. I know they think I'm crazy, that they're afraid of me. But I'm not crazy. I'm not. I know what I see, what I hear. I know what's real.

But even as I say that, I can feel the doubt creeping in, the fear that maybe I am losing my mind, that maybe everything I believe is a lie. It's a terrifying thought, and I can't shake it.

I don't know how much longer I can hold on. I'm tired—so tired—of fighting, of struggling against the darkness that's consuming me. I don't want to live like this anymore, trapped in a mind that's turned against me.

14th August, I've made a decision. It's the only way out, the only way to end this nightmare. I can't live like this anymore, trapped in a mind that's become a prison, a torture chamber. I can't go on hearing the voices, feeling the eyes on me, knowing that I'm slowly losing my grip on reality.

I've written a final poem, a farewell to the world I once loved, to the life I once cherished. It's a poem of despair, of resignation, of surrender. It's a poem that says goodbye, in the only way I know how.

The gun is on the desk in front of me. It's cold, heavy, a tool of finality. I've thought about this for a long time, and now, at last, I'm ready. I'm not afraid anymore. The voices have fallen silent, the shadows have receded. There's only the quiet now, a peaceful, empty quiet.

I don't know what comes next, but I hope it's an end to the fear, to the madness, to the torment. I hope it's a release, a final escape from the prison of my mind.

Goodbye, world. Goodbye, Ellen. I'm sorry.

15

The words blur on the page as my breathing quickens, each word sinking like a knife into my chest. The room around me starts to spin, and my vision narrows until all I can see are the jagged, tormenting lines of my father's final words. His pain, his fear, it's all too much.

I gasp for air, but it feels like there's none left in the room. My heart is pounding in my ears, a deafening drumbeat that drowns out everything else. My hands are trembling, the journal slipping from my fingers as I stumble backward. I try to hold on, to ground myself, but it's like the walls are closing in on me, crushing me under the weight of his words.

I can't breathe. I can't think. I can't—

The panic hits me like a tidal wave, pulling me under, dragging me into a whirlpool of terror and confusion. My father's voice, his pain, echoes in my mind, a haunting me. I feel like I'm drowning in his despair, sinking deeper and deeper into the darkness that swallowed him whole.

I collapse onto the floor, curling into a ball as I try to make myself as small as possible, to disappear. Tears stream down my face, but I don't even notice them. All I can feel is the crushing weight on my chest, the suffocating grip of fear that won't let me go.

My father is gone. He's gone, and I'm left here, alone, to face the demons that drove him to the edge. I can't do this. I can't bear it. The world feels too big, too terrifying, and I'm too small, too fragile.

I don't know how long I lie there, curled up on the cold floor, gasping for air and clutching at my chest as if I can stop my heart from shattering. Time loses all meaning. It's just me and the darkness, me and the crushing weight of everything I've just read.

Finally, the panic begins to recede, leaving me feeling hollow, drained. My breathing slows, but my chest still aches, a dull, persistent pain that won't go away. I force myself to sit up, to wipe the tears from my face, but the room feels foreign, like I'm seeing it for the first time through a haze of grief and confusion.

I look down at the journal lying open on the floor, the pages stained with my tears. My father's words stare back at me.

I pick up the journal with trembling hands, my fingers tracing the lines of his final lines. How could I not have seen it? How could I not have known how much he was suffering? The guilt crashes over me in waves, threatening to pull me under again, but I fight it, clutching the journal to my chest like a lifeline.

I take a deep, shuddering breath, trying to steady myself. My father is gone, but his words are still here, a piece of him that he left behind. And I can't let his pain, his fear, his final moments define him. I can't let them define me.

But right now, in this moment, it's hard to see anything else. It's hard to see past the darkness that's threatening to swallow me whole, the darkness that took him away from me.

I sit there, clutching the journal, trying to find some semblance of strength in the midst of my fear. I don't know how I'm going to get through this, how I'm going to carry the weight of his words. But I know I have to try.

For him. For me. For the father I lost, and the girl who's still trying to find her way out of the darkness.

The sunlight was fading away, I packed my backpack with the dairy and started to run to my home from wooden cabin, I want to confess about the book to my mother.

I kept on running till I reach my home.

I knocked the door, my mother opened the door, i gasped in short breathe, I was about to speak to her, but I fainted into her, cause It's been days I ate a proper meal.

16

I woke up in my bedroom feeling exhausted. As I reached for my backpack to check on the book I had brought, I realized it was missing. Just as I was about to go outside, I heard my mother's voice, trembling as she spoke to my uncle.

"She read the book she wrote," my mother said, her voice filled with fear.

"I advised you to tell her earlier. She's suffering from Split Personality Disorder; she should have known about it sooner," my uncle replied, his tone harsh.

"I'm so terrified that I might lose my daughter the same way I lost my husband," my mother cried.

Those words struck me deeply. Was I the one who had written those stories filled with pain? Anger and fear surged within me. Was I a terrible person?

In tears, I grabbed my phone and wrote:

"*The realization hit me like a freight train, leaving me breathless and disoriented. The fragments of my shattered psyche scattered before me, and a deep, paralyzing fear took root in my chest. I had always been haunted by the uncertainty of my split personality disorder, a relentless shadow that lurked just out of sight, waiting to strike.*

My breathing grew shallow, each inhale more ragged than the last. My mind raced with a whirlwind of thoughts—each fragment of my fractured self screaming for attention, each voice battling for dominance. It was as if the book had unlocked a door to a part of my psyche I wasn't ready to face. I had spent so long trying to keep the different facets of my personality at bay, only to find them swirling around me in a chaotic dance of despair.

In the midst of this overwhelming fear, I felt a creeping numbness, a coldness spreading through me that I couldn't ignore. My vision blurred, and the room seemed to close in around me. The very thought that this disorder could ultimately be my undoing was almost too much to bear. The anxiety was suffocating, wrapping around me like a vise, squeezing the breath from my lungs.

As the world around me began to fade, my mind felt detached, drifting away from the confines of my own body. The fear, the struggle, and the overwhelming weight of my own condition all converged in a final, devastating crescendo. It was as if my soul was being pulled into an abyss from which there was no return."

I looked at myself in the mirror, terrified of the disordered figure staring back. A voice echoed in my mind: "What's the point of living? People will be scared of you anyway." The words sent a chill down my spine.

In a state of despair, I threw my phone aside. I wanted to end the paradox within me. I reached for the knife I had hidden under my bed and made several cuts on my wrist. As my vision blurred and the pain slowly began to register, I remembered moments with my father, sitting by the campfire, eating roasted marshmallows. I smiled faintly, then closed my eyes, surrendering to the darkness.

Remember those moments with my father where I sat in front campfire and ate roasted marshmallows. I smiled and closed my eyes forever.

STORY-WRITING COMPETITION

"You would never know how hard life can turn cruel again and again until the day you lose hope completely. It's like a situation where your generation of people doesn't even understand how hard life can be. To be clear, your generation can't even imagine the hardships we faced.

Do you have any idea how it feels when the person you admire all your life is killed in front of you, and it's said that the person was the cruelest human ever alive?" he shouted at me.

"It felt like a thousand arrows hit me. I wanted to fight back because I wanted to prove that I was the main villain in this story. But even I didn't want to fight because I was a hero to many people who trusted me," his eyes turned red with anger while he screamed, and tears accompanied him.

I left the house immediately without uttering a single word. My father didn't speak to me either. I wanted to visit my friend. I went to her house, noticing the doors weren't locked. I sat on the couch, waiting for her.

She rushed upstairs, tears falling from her eyes over her cheeks. I was so afraid to check on her. I was worried my imagination of her smiley would be spoiled, I thought she just needed a bit of her time, so I left the house without any word with her. It's been 40 minutes since I left the house, I wanted to run back to her I didn't want to disturb her comfort zone with my presence.

I have decided to visit her. I opened the door, which I regret my entire life. I sense the glum atmosphere over the rooms. I went upstairs to her room, I was worried about her. I opened the door, to see her lying on the floor with cuts all over her wrist and a shattered mirror near her body. I have trembled to the floor, The moment a wave of regret washed over my face. Tears out of my eyes, felt like this wasn't really... I have observed her diary lying on the table with the title "Trapped"

"I sulked in my room for days, not days but months...

The thoughts in my mind are flooding. I just stayed in my home and now this four-sided room makes turmoil within me, but going out even scares me. It's like I live with entirely emotionless people. I just got stuck here, where being kind to people is an unbearable offence. I just don't want to live in this world. I'm tired of acting for people.

I'm tired of people

I'm tired of the list of people, so-called friends, who just pretend all the time.

I'm so tired of myself...

I just want to run away from myself..."

That was her last diary entry...

"May you find peace in heaven," I whispered as I closed the coffin for the last time, tears streaming down my face. I was overcome with a trembling grief that felt as if it might consume me.

"Do you have regrets, my son?" he asked, his voice laced with the anger of a child.

I had never seen my father with such a look of anguish before. His words cut through me like a knife: "I was always a coward, hiding in the shadow of someone strong and brave. I lied to many, promising to protect them, only to end up hurting them instead," I replied.

I cried as my father comforted me, his words piercing through my heart.

Epilogue

The moment my mother and uncle entered the room, their faces were engrave with disbelief and dread. My mother, overwhelmed by the weight of her grief, collapsed to the ground. The loss had hit her hardest; she had endured the deaths of her own parents, her beloved husband, and now her daughter.

In that moment, I reflected on her strength. Despite everything, she had carried on, managing her pain with a stoic resolve. I had won the essay competition, but at what cost? My life had been the price of my achievement. Life's twists are often unpredictable, and in just four short days, everything had unraveled.

We can never truly predict how life will unfold. The story that had dominated these few days had left us all changed, and the future remained an uncertain enigma.

The last story in the diary was meant to be none other than the journey of Ellen Brown, right up until her death.